POST

To the sponsors of the First Baptist Church of Decatur,
Georgia, who said, "Come in!" to hundreds
of refugees—my family among them.
And to Ruby, Sam, Grace, Brady, and Chloe.
—C. A. D.

To David and Aylene Calnan,
masters of the art of hospitality.
—B. L.

Ω

Published by Margaret Quinlin Books
An imprint of PEACHTREE PUBLISHING COMPANY INC.
1700 Chattahoochee Avenue
Atlanta, Georgia 30318
PeachtreeBooks.com

Title lettering by Adela Pons

The illustrations were rendered in acrylics and colored pencil on Strathmore paper.

Edited by Margaret Quinlin
Design and composition by Adela Pons

Printed and bound in June 2022 at Toppan Leefung, DongGuan, China.
10 9 8 7 6 5 4 3 2 1
First Edition
ISBN: 978-1-68263-321-2

Cataloging-in-Publication Data is available from the Library of Congress.

ACKNOWLEDGMENTS

Special thanks to my husband and best friend, John, who is never too busy to listen to a new story. And to Ted Egan and Nerys Evans of Alice Springs, Australia, for offering many helpful comments and insights.
—C. A. D

WOMBAT SAID COME IN

CARMEN AGRA DEEDY

Illustrated by

BRIAN LIES

Margaret Quinlin Books

PEACHTREE

ATLANTA

Wombat was not worried.

No, not a tittle. Fire had passed over his burrow before.

Best, he thought, *to shelter under my crazy quilt until the trouble passes.*

But, as it often does, trouble came knocking . . .

"Walleeooooo, Wombat!"

Outside was his friend Wallaby, eyes wide with fright. "Help, Wombat! I c-c-can't reach my home! M-m-may I stay with you awhile?"

Wombat hesitated only for one tick of the clock.

Then . . .

Wombat said, "Come in!"
Wombat said, "Come in!
From smoke and din
and howling wind,
come in, my friend, come in!"

A grateful Wallaby hopped inside and was soon twitching in his sleep under a certain crazy quilt.

No worries, thought Wombat, *I'll have a cup of tea in my favorite chair instead.*

But as he lowered himself into that chair, he heard,

“Woo-hoo-ha-ha-ha!”

Kookaburra was at the door. He looked scorched and bad-tempered. "Dreadful out here, Wombat! Fire is on the march. Spare a room for an old friend?"

I do have quite a few rooms, thought Wombat.

And so . . .

Wombat said, “Come in!”
Wombat said, “Come in!
From smoke and din
and howling wind,
come in, my friend, come in!”

With a laugh of purest joy, Kookaburra commandeered Wombat's favorite chair.

"Kettle on, Wombat? Could do with some tea."

Where are my manners? thought Wombat.
Before he could fetch his slippers, he heard,

"Help! I can't—*ah-chooo!*"

Without warning, in tumbled Platypus,
and out of Platypus tumbled a jumble of words.

"Wombat, I can't find my way and I've lost my shoe and there's smoke in my nostrils and . . ."

Wombat patted his pockets for a handkerchief. He found three. Platypus took them all.

"May I stay with you, dear Wombat? It's sooooooo hot. Heat! Hotness! Oh, the hot-hot-hotness of it all!"

How, thought Wombat, *does Platypus talk so much and say so little?*

There was only one thing Wombat could think to do.

Wombat said, "Come in!"
Wombat said, "Come in!
From smoke and din
and howling wind,
come in, my friend, come in!"

"Already in!" said Platypus, then she brightened. "Ooooo, slippers!"

As Platypus padded away in Wombat's favorite slippers, she trilled, "Tea and toast, please, Wombat! I'll be in my room!"

Tea does make a hard day easier to bear, thought Wombat.

His clock chimed in agreement.

But you've already guessed that poor Wombat didn't finish preparing that tea and toast.

"Help!"

Wombat rushed toward the cry.

"Stuck," gasped Koala, as he tugged on a sooty eucalyptus branch.

Sounding a bit less friendly than he intended . . .

Wombat said, "Come in!"
Wombat said, "Come in!
From smoke and din
and howling wind,
come in, my friend, come in!"

"But leave that smelly twig outside," he muttered.

"Not smelly," corrected Koala as he gave the branch a yank.

It plowed into the burrow, and down went the clock with a *clang-lang-lang.*

This day, worried Wombat, *is getting quite out of hand.*

"You'd like tea, I suppose," he huffed.

"No thanks," murmured Koala. "Only 'lyptus."

Well, I *must have tea,* thought Wombat, *with three—no, FOUR—lumps of sugar.*

This sweet thought restored Wombat to his best self. But then he heard . . .

"Wombat-bat!"

"Sugar Glider?"

"Fire-fire," squeaked Sugar Glider. "Come in-in?"

Oh well, what's one more? thought Wombat.

So . . .

Wombat said, "Come in!"
Wombat said, "Come in!
From smoke and din
and howling wind,
come in, my fr—"

THWACK!

Sugar Glider took
a flying leap onto
Wombat's snout.

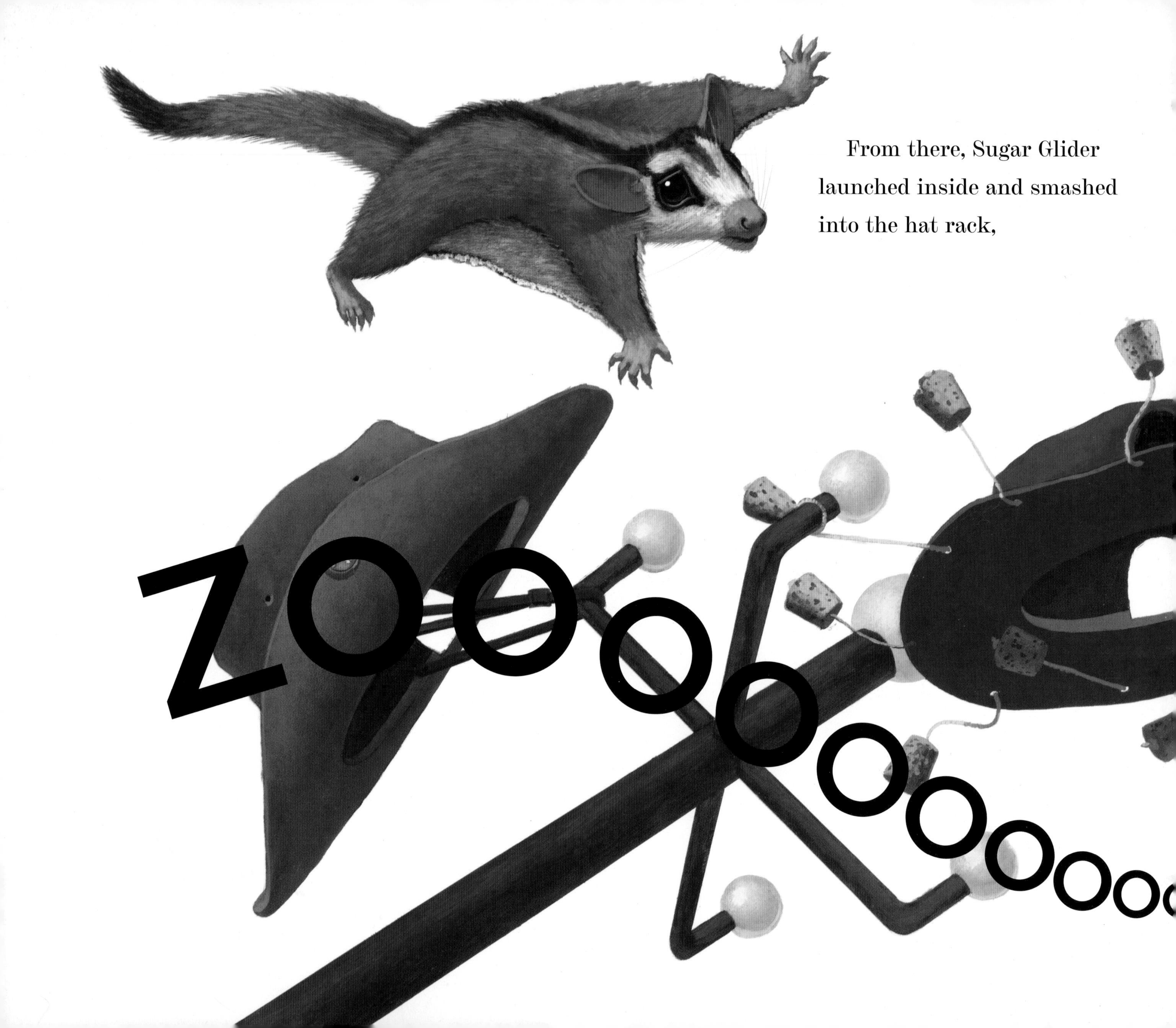

From there, Sugar Glider launched inside and smashed into the hat rack,

from which he fell onto a nearby tea tray, where he tipped over a bowl of sugar cubes.

"Sugar Glider! Do NOT TOUCH—"

Too late.

Sugar Glider had snarfled up every last sugar cube.

Wombat did not trust himself to speak.

Seeing his distress, Sugar Glider leapt onto Wombat's shirt, pulled a gooey cube from his mouth, and dropped it into Wombat's paw.

Then he scrabbled into a pocket. "Sleep-sleep," he cooed.

Wombat studied the sticky gift and thought, *What an odd day this has been. But they'll surely go home soon.*

Wombat was mistaken.

ARRIER REEF
IDE
ANNED
ERRIES
Mel

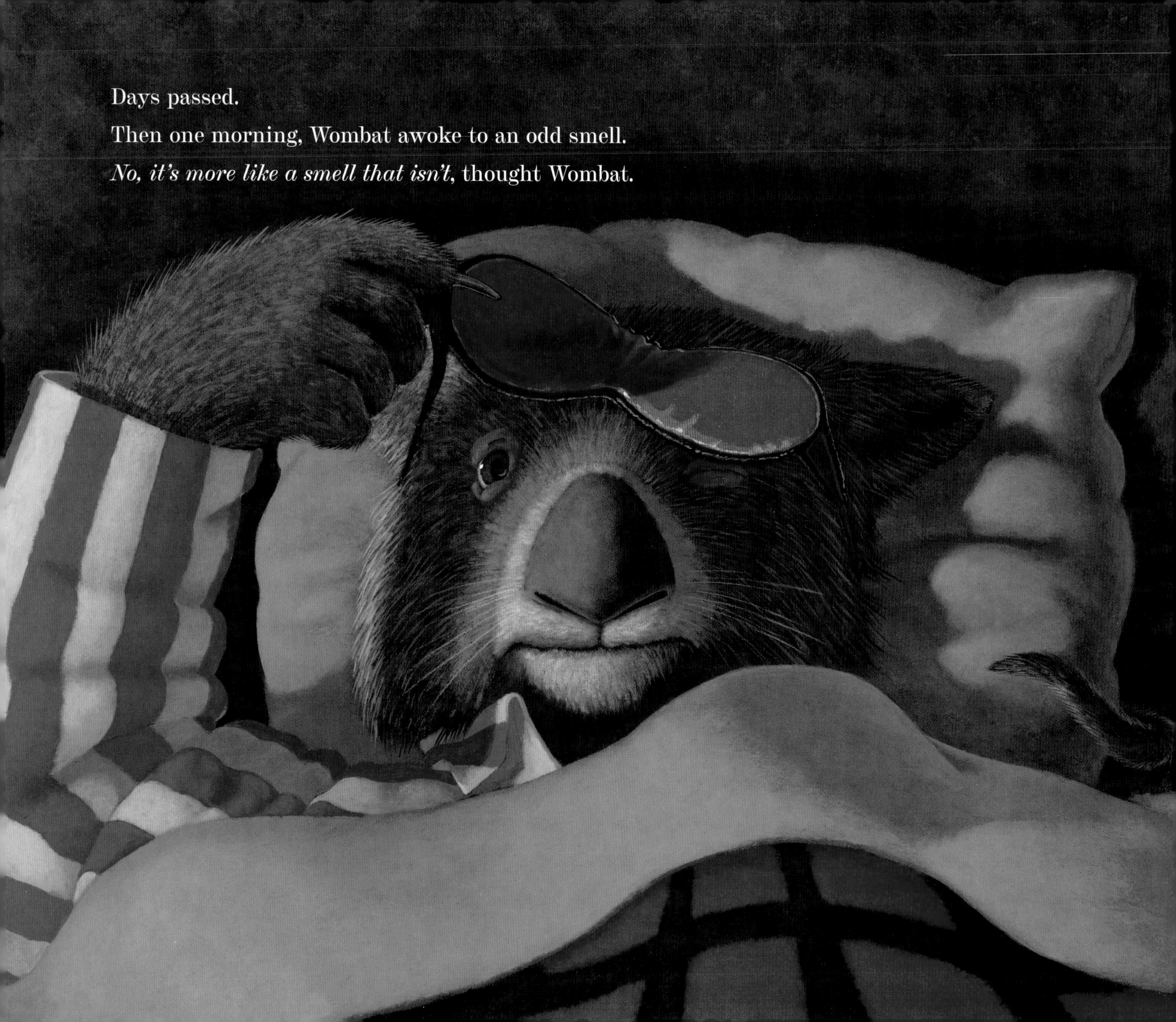

Days passed.

Then one morning, Wombat awoke to an odd smell.

No, it's more like a smell that isn't, thought Wombat.

He tiptoed past his sleeping guests
and peeked outside the burrow.

The smoke had cleared.
The ground was cool.

So . . .

Wombat said, "Go home!"

Wombat said, "GO HOME!

It's safe for you to rove and roam,

and time for me to be alone.

Skedaddle! Shoo! *Go home!*"

"Thank you-you," said a small voice.

Wombat frowned as he plucked Sugar Glider from his pocket.

"GO. HOME."

Sugar Glider sighed.

"No home-home to go to-to."

Wombat's ears twitched.

He clacked his teeth.

He made an odd whickering sound.

And finally . . .

Wombat said, “*Come in.*”

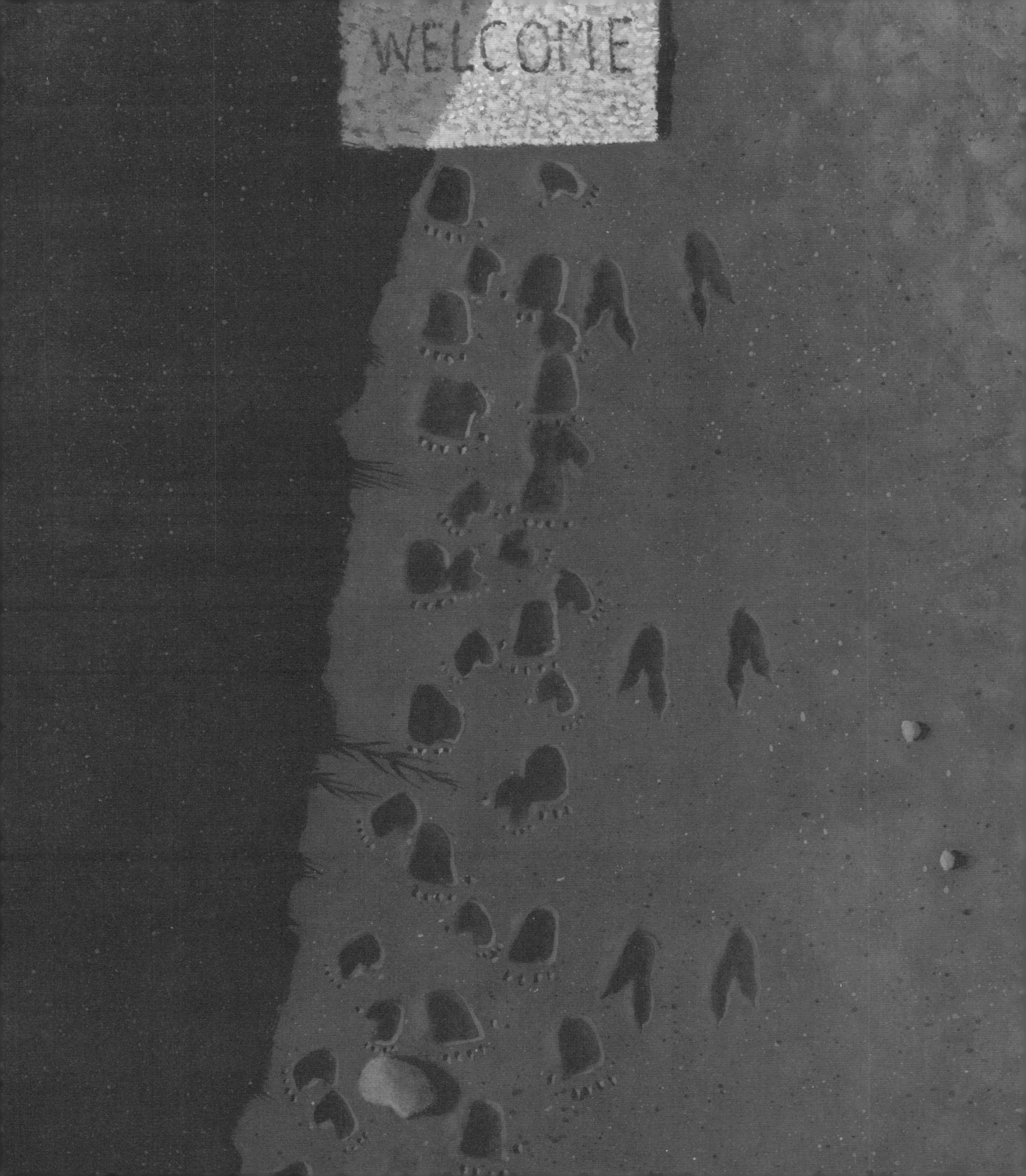
WELCOME